First edition

Published by Ladybird Books Ltd Loughborough Leicestershire UK

© 1991 THE WALT DISNEY COMPANY
Printed in England (3)

DISNEY
ALICE IN WONDERLAND

Ladybird Books

One sunny summer afternoon, a girl named Alice sat in a tree with her cat, Dinah. Alice was supposed to be listening to her older sister reading a history lesson, but she couldn't keep her mind on it. Her thoughts kept drifting to other things.

At last Alice climbed down from the tree. In a dreamy mood, she wandered off with Dinah.

Alice was lost in thought when a white rabbit scurried by. Suddenly Alice's eyes opened wide. This was no ordinary rabbit – it was wearing a jacket and waistcoat! And it was carrying a big pocket-watch!

"Mr Rabbit, wait!" called Alice, running after him.

"I'm late! I'm late!" cried the rabbit. Before Alice could catch up with him, he had disappeared into a hole at the foot of the tree.

Alice decided to follow him. She crawled into the hole, and all at once she was falling down into the darkness.

Furniture, pictures, mirrors and lamps all floated past her as she fell.

When at last she landed, Alice saw the White Rabbit hurrying down a corridor. He slipped through a tiny door.

"Curiouser and curiouser!" Alice said to herself.

Alice knelt by the door and tried to peep through the keyhole.

"Oh! You gave me quite a turn!" said a voice.

Alice sprang back in surprise. The doorknob had spoken!

"Well, one good turn deserves another," the doorknob went on. "What can I do for you?"

"I was following a White Rabbit," Alice replied, "but I'll never fit through this door."

"Try the bottle on the table," said the doorknob.

11

DRINK ME

Alice looked on the table and saw a small bottle with a tag that said *Drink Me*. She uncorked the bottle and drank some of the liquid in it.

She quickly began to shrink, and soon she was little enough to get through the door.

On the other side of
the door Alice found
herself in Wonderland.
It was an amazing
place. There were birds
that talked, fish that
danced, and two egg-
shaped men called Tweedle
Dee and Tweedle Dum.

Alice made her way through
a wood until she came to a
cottage. "I wonder who lives
there?" she thought.

A window flew open, and
the White Rabbit appeared.
He was wearing a tunic
with a big ruffled collar.

"There you are!" he
shouted at Alice. "Go
get my gloves! I'm late!"

"He must think I'm his
maid," thought Alice
as she went inside.

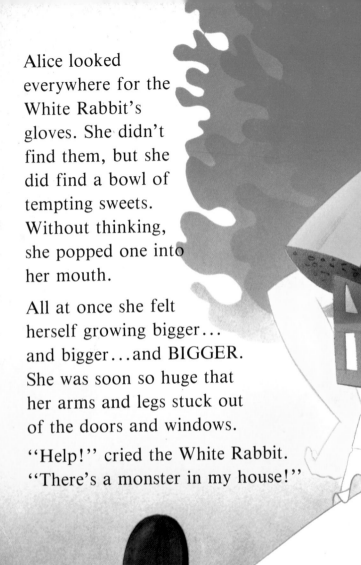

Alice looked
everywhere for the
White Rabbit's
gloves. She didn't
find them, but she
did find a bowl of
tempting sweets.
Without thinking,
she popped one into
her mouth.

All at once she felt
herself growing bigger...
and bigger...and BIGGER.
She was soon so huge that
her arms and legs stuck out
of the doors and windows.

"Help!" cried the White Rabbit.
"There's a monster in my house!"

Alice had to do something quickly.
She seemed to change size every time
she ate or drank something, so she
reached down and picked a carrot
from the White Rabbit's garden.

It worked. As soon as she took a bite of the carrot, Alice grew small again.

The White Rabbit had run off into the wood, and Alice hurried after him. But now she was so tiny that she couldn't keep up with him!

Alice was wondering what to do when she saw an odd-looking caterpillar sitting on a mushroom. He was puffing on a water pipe and blowing smoke rings into the air. "*Who* are *you*?" he asked Alice.

"I'm not sure myself," Alice replied. "But I do wish I were a little taller!"

"Then I'll tell you this," said the Caterpillar. "One side will make you grow taller, and the other side will make you grow shorter."

"One side of what?" asked Alice.

"This mushroom, of course!"
said the Caterpillar.
Then, in a puff of
smoke, he turned
into a butterfly
and flew away.

Alice didn't know which side of the mushroom did what, and the only way to find out was to try some. She broke off a few bits and tasted one. Before she knew it, her head was high above the treetops and a bird had built its nest in her hair.

"This won't do," thought Alice, and she popped a piece from the other side of the mushroom into her mouth. In seconds she was her normal size again. She put some bits of mushroom in her pocket, just in case she ever needed them again.

Then Alice came across a very strange
creature – a Cheshire Cat.

"Hello," said Alice. "Have you seen
the White Rabbit?"

"He might be with the March Hare and
the Mad Hatter," said the Cheshire Cat.
"They went *that* way," he added, taking
off his head the way anyone else would
take off a hat. Then he disappeared,
leaving only his smile behind.

The Mad Hatter
and the March
Hare were having
a tea party when
Alice found them.

"Welcome to our un-birthday party!" said the Mad Hatter.

"What's an un-birthday?" asked Alice.

"Why, any day that's not your birthday, of course!" said the Mad Hatter.

"Then it's *my* un-birthday!" said Alice.

The Mad Hatter brought Alice an un-birthday cake, but it exploded when she blew out the candle. Alice decided it was time to leave.

Alice had had enough of Wonderland. All she wanted now was to go home. But she couldn't find her way out of the wood.

Then, just when she had found a path to follow, a dog with a broom for a head came along and swept the path away.

Poor Alice! How would she ever get home now? She sat down and began to cry.

"You must go to the Queen," said a voice.

Alice looked up. There, sitting in a big tree, was the Cheshire Cat. Alice was so glad to see him!

"I'll show you the Short Cut," he said. He pulled at a branch, and the trunk of the tree opened like a door.

In front of Alice was a long path with tall hedges on either side. At the end of the path was the Queen's palace. Alice walked towards it.

Suddenly two long lines of playing cards
marched past, carrying spears. Alice
knew they must be the Queen's guards.
The Queen herself would soon be here.

Then someone blew a trumpet. It was the White Rabbit! Alice had found him after all!

"Her Royal Majesty, the Queen of Hearts!" he announced.

At last the Queen arrived. She seemed nasty and bad-tempered.

"Who are you?" she barked at Alice.

"I'm Alice, your Majesty," Alice replied, curtseying. "I've lost my way."

"*Your* way?" roared the Queen. "All the ways round here belong to *me*!" Then, in a softer voice, she asked, "Do you play croquet?"

"Yes, your Majesty," said Alice.

"Then we must have a game!" declared
the Queen.

It was the strangest game of croquet Alice had ever seen. The mallets were flamingos, the balls were hedgehogs and the hoops were the Queen's playing-card guards. They all knew the Queen would be terribly angry if she lost the game, so they made sure her ball went through the hoops every time.

But the clumsy Queen tripped over her own mallet, and went head over heels onto the lawn.

She was furious, of course, and needed someone to blame. "You!" she shouted at Alice. "Off with your head!"

The King of Hearts persuaded the Queen to hold a trial first, so Alice was marched into an enormous courtroom. She was charged with annoying the Queen and making her lose her temper.

Witnesses were called, but they made
no difference to the Queen. "Off with
her head!" she roared from her
throne.

Alice was very worried – until she
remembered the bits of magic
mushroom in her pocket. She took out
a piece and bit into it...

Suddenly Alice was gigantic, towering over the Queen and everyone else.

"Er...can't we be friends?" stammered the Queen in a frightened voice.

"Friends with you?" said Alice. "Why, you're nothing but an ugly, bad-tempered old woman!" As she said the words, Alice began shrinking back to her normal size.

"Off with her head!" shrieked the Queen, as soon as Alice was small again.

Alice fled. The Queen's guards ran after her, and chased her into a maze. Everywhere she turned, she saw angry guards coming at her.

Alice escaped from
the maze at last,
but the Queen and
her guards were
close behind.
Alice ran and
ran, until she
was in front of
the tiny door
once more.

She looked
through the
keyhole and saw
– herself, asleep
under a tree! She
could hear a familiar
voice calling her name.

Alice opened her eyes.
There was her sister. And
there was Dinah, her cat.

Her adventures in Wonderland
had all been a fantastic dream.

Or had they?